Book Club Edition

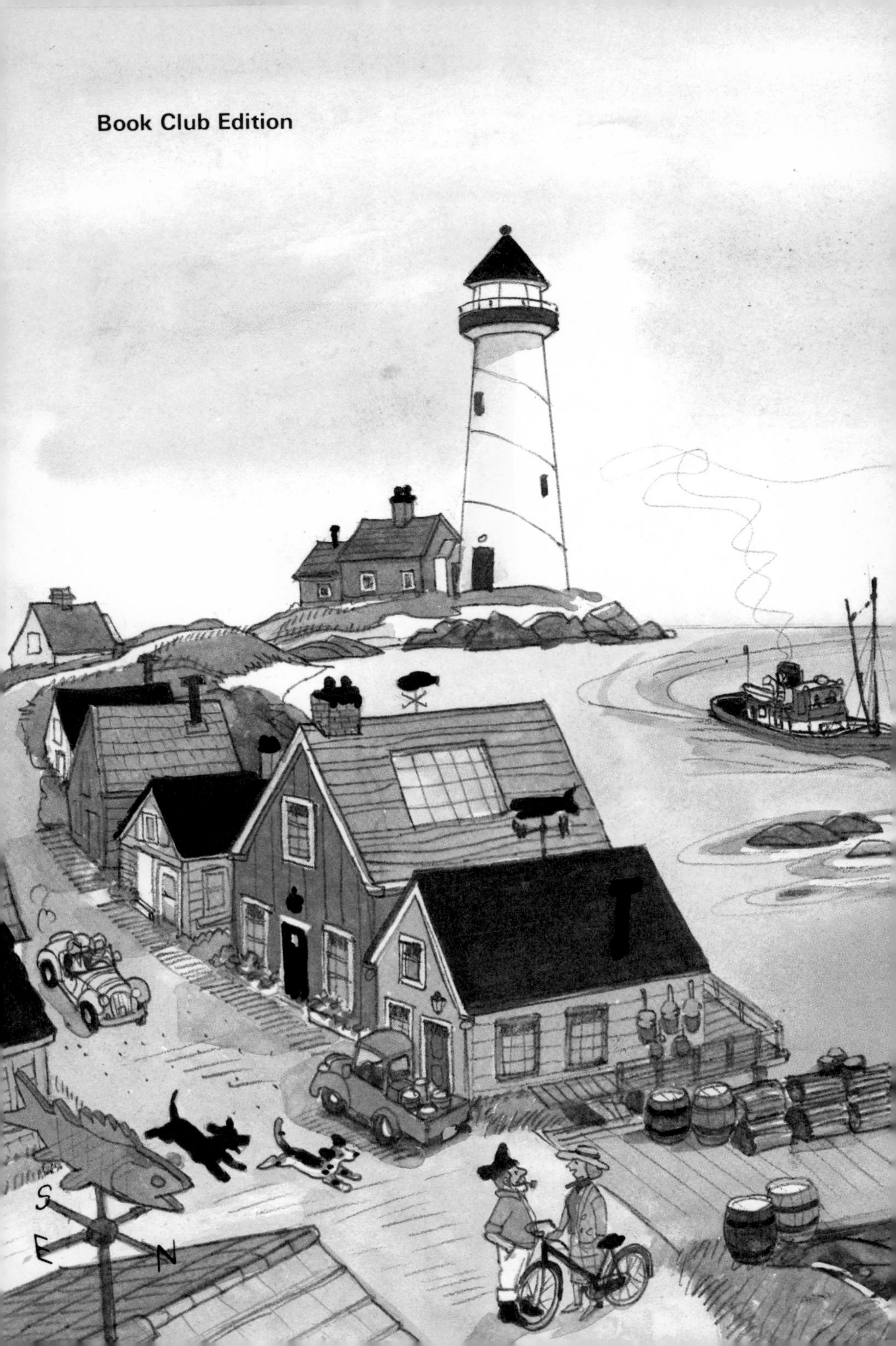

WALT DISNEY PRODUCTIONS

presents

Donald Duck's Birthday

Random House New York

First American Edition. Copyright © 1984 by Walt Disney Productions. All rights reserved under International and Pan-American Copyright Conventions. Published in the United States by Random House, Inc., New York, and simultaneously in Canada by Random House of Canada Limited, Toronto. Originally published in Denmark as ANDERS ANDS FOEDSELSDAG by Gutenberghus Gruppen, Copenhagen. ISBN: 0-394-86597-9   Manufactured in the United States of America

4 5 6 7 8 9 0   A B C D E F G H I J K

The first day of the summer
fishing season was warm and sunny.
Donald Duck had been waiting
for this day.
Out he went in his red motor boat.
The fish were really biting!
Donald had a wonderful time
that morning.

In the afternoon, dark clouds appeared.
"I'll just land one more fish,"
said Donald. "Then I'll head
ashore."
Soon it began to rain.

"There's no time to lose!"
said Donald.
   He hauled in the anchor.
   The wind was blowing very hard.

Donald's boat was tossed on the waves.

There was thunder and lightning.
Donald tried to steer toward shore.

Donald Duck's nephews watched their uncle.
Huey, Dewey, and Louie were worried.
"I hope Uncle Donald sees those rocks
in the water!" said Dewey.

SMASH! went the boat onto the rocks.
Donald and the fish flew out of the boat.
Donald was not far from shore, so
the boys dragged him up onto the beach.
"Poor Uncle Donald!" said Huey.

Donald and his nephews looked at
the remains of the boat.

All they could see were broken planks.
Then Louie found Donald's fishing rod.

"This won't do me any good now,"
said Donald sadly.

There was nothing to do but go home.

"Some fishing season this turned out to be," said Donald. "I don't have a boat or a rod. I don't even have any fish."
He looked very glum.

"You're lucky to be safe," said Dewey.
"You didn't wear your life jacket."
But Donald just sat in his chair,
looking sadly at the rain through the window.
The boys went upstairs to their room.

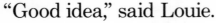

"We have to cheer up Uncle Donald," said Dewey.

"His birthday is soon," said Huey.

"Maybe we can buy him a new boat with the money in our banks," said Dewey.

"Good idea," said Louie.

Dewey broke his piggy bank with a hammer.
"Look at all those coins!" Dewey said.
"My turn!" said Louie, and he grabbed
the hammer.
"Me next, me next!" said Huey.

Donald heard crashing sounds.
"I wonder what those boys
are up to," he said.

So he tiptoed up the stairs.

Donald peeked into the boys' room.
He saw them happily counting their money.
"Isn't that nice," Donald thought.
"They must be planning a surprise for me."

Soon the boys set off with their money.
"Hope we find a nice boat," said Louie.
On the way to town
they met Uncle Scrooge.
"What are you boys up to?"
asked Uncle Scrooge.

"Uncle Donald wrecked
his boat," said Dewey.

"So we're going to buy him
a new one," said Louie.

"For his birthday," said Huey.

"Hmm," said Uncle Scrooge.
"I'd like to see that."

So he went along with them
to the sports store.

There were wonderful things
in the store!
"Look at those engines,"
said Louie.
"And this diving gear,"
said Uncle Scrooge.
Dewey spotted a big motorboat.
"This is just the boat for
Uncle Donald," he said.

"Just think of the fun we'd have!"
said Louie.

"What do you say, Uncle Scrooge?"
asked Dewey.

"It's your money, boys," said
Uncle Scrooge. "Ask the sales clerk."

Huey, Dewey, and Louie
showed the sales clerk
their coins.

"Is this enough?" they said.

"Hmm," said the salesman. "That might
pay for the steering wheel, but not
the boat. Sorry, boys."

Huey, Dewey, and Louie looked very sad.

FISHING RODS FOR SALE
BUY ONE AND GET
A BAMBOO POLE FREE

"How about a fishing rod?" the salesman said. "Buy a rod and you get a bamboo pole free. But for you boys, I'll make it three bamboo poles."

"Hmm, that's an idea," said Dewey.

Just then Uncle Scrooge saw another sign.

SPECIAL OFFER

BUILD-IT-YOURSELF BOAT KIT

ONLY
A FEW
LEFT!

"A build-it-yourself boat kit would be fun for the boys," said Uncle Scrooge, reading the sign.

So he called them over.

"If you're willing to build a boat,
I'll pay for the kit," Uncle Scrooge said.
"That boat looks great!" said Huey.
"It will be a lot of work," said Dewey.
"But I'm sure we can do it," said Louie.

So Uncle Scrooge bought the kit and
the boys bought the fishing rod.

"We want the gifts to be a surprise,"
said Huey. "Please send them to
our friend Mickey's house."

Then the boys went home with their poles.

Donald was peeking out
the window as the boys came
home from their shopping trip.
He saw them pass by with
their new bamboo fishing poles.

Then the boys walked
to the garage to hide
their poles.

"Those ungrateful scamps!"
Donald said. "They've spent
all their money on themselves!"

He stamped his foot.
"They've forgotten
all about my birthday!"
he said angrily.

Early the next morning the boys went
over to Mickey Mouse's house.
They started unpacking the boat kit.

Mickey helped them to read
the instructions.

Minnie brought them lemonade.

Huey, Dewey, and Louie
worked on the boat every day.
It was really taking shape!

Soon it was the day before Donald's birthday.

The only thing left to do was to paint the boat.

"Today's my birthday!" Donald said
the next morning when he woke up. "I'm
sure the boys have some surprise for me!"

So he rushed out
of bed to look
for the boys.
   The house was
very quiet.

Donald looked in the boys' bedroom.
Their beds were empty.
He hurried downstairs.
There was a note on the kitchen table.

"Happy Birthday,
Uncle Donald. Sorry
we can't spend the day
with you," he read.

"Hmph!" said Donald.
"I guess those boys
are just too busy with
more important things."

Just then
the doorbell rang.
"I wonder who that
can be," Donald said
to himself.

Minnie Mouse was at the door.
"Happy Birthday, Donald," she said.
"Mickey and I wanted you to come over."
"I'm glad SOMEONE cares," Donald said.

Soon they were
on their way.

All of Donald's friends were waiting
outside Mickey's house.
"Happy Birthday!" they cried.
Donald felt much better.

"Happy Birthday, Uncle Donald!" said
Huey, Dewey, and Louie.

They gave him the fine new fishing rod.
Then Minnie gave him an outboard motor.
"But I don't have a boat," said Donald.
"Oh, yes you do!" said Mickey. "Look!"

Mickey led Donald to the back yard.
There sat the new boat!
"The boys made this for you
from a boat kit," Mickey said.

"Those boys are good workers,"
Uncle Scrooge said to Donald. "You
can be very proud of them."

That very same day Uncle Scrooge,
Donald, and the boys went fishing in
the brand-new boat.

It was the best fishing trip they
had ever had!